MARY JONES
& HER BIBLE

Children's Victorian Classics

MARY JONES
& HER BIBLE

by M.E.R (Mary Ropes)
Revised & Updated by Christopher Wright

Bridge-Logos *Publishers*

North Brunswick, New Jersey 08902 USA

Also available in the Children's Victorian Classics series:

At the Back of North Wind by John Bunyan
Christiana's Journey by John Bunyan
Young Christian's Pilgrimage by John Bunyan
Target Earth! by John Bunyan
Christie's Old Organ by Mrs. 0. F. Walton
A Peep Behind the Scenes by Mrs. 0. F. Walton
The Rocky Island & Other Stories by Wilberforce & Gatty

Copyright © 1985 Christopher Wright
New Edition 2000
by Bridge-Logos Publishers
International Standard Book Number: 0-88270-789-2
Library of Congress Catalog Card Number: 99-69699

Published By:
Bridge-Logos Publishers
1300 Airport Road, Suite E
North Brunswick, NJ 08902
http://www.bridgelogos.com

CONTENTS

INTRODUCTION

This is a true story, showing how much God needs ordinary people. As the story unfolds, you will see how a girl here, a preacher there, a schoolmaster who couldn't read or write—and other people—were slowly being drawn together to start something that just couldn't be stopped.

All over the world today people are busy translating the Bible into different languages. Other people are distributing copies of it. The Bible Societies print and distribute over 300 *million* copies of the Scriptures each *year!*

The English verses used in this book have been taken from the Good News Bible, which is the version published by the Bible Societies. The Welsh verses are from an old Welsh Bible and are the exact words that Mary Jones knew.

You can still see the remains of Mary Jones' cottage, Ty'nyddol, if you go to Llanfihangel. Go past the church and quite a long way on until you come to a small bridge over the river. The public road comes to an end just here.

Although the cottage is in ruins, the lower part of the walls has been preserved and a stone monument has been built inside. The most interesting part to me is the large old fireplace which is still complete. The river runs at the back of Ty'nyddol just as it did when Mary Jones lived there. The whole area is so unchanged that you will see things just as she saw them.

Step now into this book, and step back 200 years in time to the country of Wales. Although the people would be speaking in Welsh, we will have to 'listen' in English! The story is told in an old-fashioned way, and I am sure you will enjoy the book as soon as you start reading.

There have been several books about Mary Jones, but I believe that this one by Mary Ropes (M. E. R.), first published in 1882 and reprinted many times, is the best. It is both interesting and challenging. Not only was Mary Jones a real person, but the story is still going on today. Will *you* be part of it?

Christopher Wright

Welsh is a very difficult language for English speaking people to pronounce. Here is a very quick guide to some of its letters.

'c' sounds like a k, as in KIT
'ch' sounds like ch in LOCH (a 'wet' sounding K)
'dd' sounds like th, as in THERE
'f' sounds like a v, as in VERY
'ff' sounds like an f, as in FAR
'g' is hard-sounding, as in GET
'll' sounds like a mixture of th and l (a hard one, this)
'u' sounds like ee, as in BEEN, but 'au' sounds like i, as in NINE in many areas
'w' is usually more like oo, as in SOON, than a normal w sound
'y' is like a u, as in UNDER, except in the last syllable when it sounds like i, as in SIT.

There are some exceptions to these pronunciations, but I did warn you that the language is difficult. Try Llanfihangel.

Cader Idris

CHAPTER 1

At the Foot of the Mountains

Mary Jones pulled her shawl tightly around her shoulders, and darted across the lane. There was no one to see her as she ran.

The night shadows had fallen around the little Welsh village of Llanfihangel. It was late autumn in 1792, and a cold wind moaned and sighed among the trees, stripping them of their leaves—now no longer bright green—whirling them round, and laying them in shivering heaps along the narrow valley.

The grey stone cottages of Llanfihangel-y-Pennant seemed to be hiding below the mountain of Cader Idris, with its dark crags and rocky precipices. Stretching away in the distance lay the faint outline of Cardigan Bay, with white breakers rolling in to dash into foam. The pale moon lit up peaked masses of cloud that looked like another ghostly Cader Idris in the sky.

Mary Jones looked back over her shoulder. A warm light shone through the windows of one of the cottages in the village. That cottage was her home. The light came from the blaze of a fire of dried driftwood in the stone hearth, and also from a rushlight, throwing its somewhat uncertain brightness upon a loom where a weaver sat at work. A bench, two or three stools, a cupboard, and a kitchen table—these, with the loom, were the only pieces of furniture.

Standing in the center of the room, a woman was dressed in a cloak and a tall black hat. "I am sorry you cannot go, Jacob," she was saying in Welsh. "You'll be missed at the chapel meeting."

"Yes, but I'm thankful that I needn't sit idle, but can still attend to my trade," replied Jacob Jones. "There's many a deal worse off than I am with a cold on my chest. But what are you waiting for, Molly? You'll be late. It must be gone six o'clock."

"I'm waiting for that child, and she's gone for the lantern," said Mary Jones, whom her husband generally called Molly, to distinguish her from their daughter who was also Mary.

Jacob smiled. "The lantern? Yes," he said, "you'll need it this dark night. 'Twas a good thought of yours, Molly, to let our Mary go with you. She does seem so eager."

"Yes, she knows already pretty nearly all that you and I can teach her of the Bible, as we learnt it, Jacob. I can remember when she was smaller she would sit on your knee on a Sunday, and hear about Abraham, Joseph, and David, and Daniel. There never was a girl like our Mary for Bible stories, or any stories, bless her. But here she is! You've been a long time getting that lantern, child, and we must hurry or we shall be late."

Mary raised a pair of bright dark eyes to her mother's face.

A Welsh Cottage

"Yes, mother," she replied, "I was long because I ran to borrow neighbor Williams's lantern. The latch of ours won't hold, and there's such a wind tonight, that I knew we should have the light blown out."

"There's a moon," said Mrs. Jones, "and I could have done without a lantern."

"Yes, but then I should have had to stay at home," answered Mary, for she knew that her father would not let her go without a light. Then she added, "And I do so love to go."

"You needn't tell me that, child," laughed Molly. "Then come along, Mary. Good-bye, Jacob."

"Good-bye, father! I wish you could come too!" cried Mary, running back to give Jacob a last hug.

"Go your way, child, and mind you remember all you can. Then you can tell me all you've learnt when you come home."

The cottage was called Ty'nyddol. Suddenly the door opened and Mary and her mother sallied out into the cold windy night.

The moon had disappeared now behind the thick dark cloud, and Mary's borrowed lantern was very useful. Carefully she held it, so that the light fell upon the way they had to go, a way which would have been difficult if not dangerous, without its friendly aid. "Llusern yw dy air i'm traed, a llewyrch i'm llwybr." said Mrs. Jones, remembering words from the Bible. "Your word is a lamp to guide me and a light for my path." Psalm 119: 105.

"Yes, mother, I was just thinking of that," replied Mary. "I wish I knew more verses like that one."

4

"How glad I should be if your father and I could teach you more. But it's years since we learned, and we've got no Bible, and our memories are not as good and they used to be," sighed Mrs. Jones.

A walk of some length along a rough road, brought them at last to the little meeting-house where the members belonging to the Methodist chapel were gathered.

They were rather late, and the mid-week service had begun, but farmer Evans made room for them on his bench.

Mary was the only child there, but she was so willing to listen and to learn that no one looking at her could have felt that she was out of place. Indeed, the members who met there had come to look upon her as one of their number and made her very welcome.

When the meeting was over, Mary relit her lantern and was ready to accompany her mother home. But farmer Evans put his great broad hand on her shoulder, saying:

"Well, my little maid! You're rather young for these meetings, though the Lord has need of lambs as well as sheep. And He is well pleased when the lambs learn to hear His voice early, even in their tender years."

Then with a gentle smile the old man released the girl, and turned away. He knew that in Mary's face there was a promise of power for good.

"Why *haven't* we a Bible of our own, mother?" asked Mary as she trotted homeward, lantern in hand.

"Because Bibles are scarce, child, and we're too poor to pay the price for one. A weaver's is an honest trade, Mary, but we don't get rich by it, and we think ourselves happy if we can keep the wolf from the door, and have clothes to cover us. Still, precious as the Word of God would be in our hands, it is more important that its teachings and its truths find a place in our hearts. I tell you, my girl, they who come to know the love of God, have discovered the greatest truth that even the Bible can teach them. And those who are trusting Jesus for their pardon and peace, and for eternal life, can wait patiently to find out more of His word and will!"

"I suppose *you* can wait, mother, because you've waited so long that you're used to it," replied Mary. "But it's harder for me. Every time I hear something read out of the Bible, I long to hear more. But if I could *read,* it would be harder still not to have one of our own!"

Mrs. Jones was about to answer, when she stumbled over a large stone, and fell, though fortunately without hurting herself. Mary's thoughts were so full of what she had been saying, that she had become careless in holding the lantern high. Her mother, not seeing the stone, had caught her foot against it. "Ah, child! It's the present duties that we must look after most!" said Molly, as she got slowly up. "And even a fall may teach us a lesson, Mary. The very Word of God itself, which is a lamp to our feet, and a light to our path, can't save us from many a tumble if we don't use it the right way. If we let the light shine on our daily life the Lord will help us in all that we do. Remember this, Mary."

And Mary did remember this, and her life proved that she had taken the lesson to heart—a simple lesson, taught by her mother who loved the Lord, and a lesson which she treasured up in her very heart of hearts. The Word of God—the Bible—the most important book in the world, and a light for the way!

CHAPTER 2

Mrs. Evans' Promise

In the homes of poor people, where the elder members of the family were needed to earn enough money for food and clothing, the children learnt to be useful very early. Girls of six or seven could take charge of a younger brother and sister, while many other children of that age ran errands, did the shopping, and made themselves of very real use for much of the day.

Such was the case in the family of Jacob Jones. Jacob and Molly were weavers of woollen cloth, so much of which used to be made in Wales. Many of the household duties became the responsibility of Mary. So, at an age when children of richer parents were amusing themselves with their toys or books, Mary was sweeping, and dusting, and scrubbing, and digging, and weeding.

It was Mary who fed the few hens, and looked for their eggs, so often laid in out-of-the-way places, rather than in the nest.

It was Mary who took care of the hive, and who never feared the bees; and it was Mary again, who, when more active duties were done, would draw a low stool towards the hearth in winter or outside the cottage door in summer and try to make or mend her own clothes. Often she would be singing to herself in Welsh a verse or two of a hymn she had learnt in chapel, or repeating texts which she had picked up and retained in her quick and eager mind.

In the long light summer evenings she chose to sit where she could see the majestic form of Cader Idris with its varying lights and shadows, as the sun sank lower and lower in the horizon. And in her imagination this mountain was made to play many a part, as she recalled the stories which her parents had told her, and the chapters she had heard read at chapel.

So Cader Idris became the mountain in the land of Moriah where Abraham was sent with Isaac. Then Mary would fix her great dark eyes upon the rocky steeps before her, until she fancied she could see Abraham and his son toiling up towards the place of sacrifice, the boy bearing the wood for the burnt offering.

More and more vividly the whole scene would grow upon her fancy, until the picture seemed to be almost a reality, and she could imagine that she heard Abraham's voice borne faintly to her ear by the breeze that fanned her cheek—a voice that replied almost sadly to his son's question, in the words, "Duw a edrych iddo ei hun am oen y poeth-offrwm." ("God Himself will provide one" Genesis 22:8).

Then the scene would change; night was drawing near and Cader Idris, taking on softer outlines, became the mountain where Jesus went to pray.

Cader Idris

Leaving the large crowd who had been trying to hear His every word—leaving even His disciples whom He loved—there was Jesus, alone save for His Father's presence, praying, and refreshing His weary spirit after the work and trials and sorrows of the day.

"If I'd only lived in those days," sighed Mary sometimes. "How I should have loved Him! *And* He'd have taught me, perhaps, as He did those two who walked such a long way with Him on the road to Emmaus, without knowing it was Jesus; only I think *I* should have known Him, just through love!"

Nor was it only the mountain of Cader ldris with which Mary associated scenes from Bible history. The long narrow valley, in the upper end of which Llanfihangel was situated, ran down to the sea by a place called Tywyn. And whenever she happened to be near, Mary would sit down on the shore, and gaze across the blue-green waters of Cardigan Bay, and dream of the Sea of Galilee, and of Jesus who walked upon its waters.

She thought of Jesus as He stilled the raging storm with a word. She thought of Him as He sometimes chose to make a boat His pulpit, and preach to the people standing upon the shore. She saw them clustered to the very edge of the water, so that they might not lose a word of the precious things that He spoke.

One afternoon Jacob and his wife were seated at their looms, and Mary was sewing a patch into an almost worn-out dress of her own. Suddenly a tap at the door of Ty'nyddol was followed by the entrance of Mrs. Evans the farmer's wife, a kind motherly woman who was looked up to and loved by many of the Llanfihangel villagers.

"Good day to you, neighbors!" she said cheerily, her face all aglow. "Jacob, how is your chest feeling? Bad, I expect, as I haven't seen you out of late. Molly, you're looking hearty as usual. And my Mary, too—I used to come here when you were small and running round on your sturdy pins as fast as many a bigger child. Don't I remember you then! You'd keep a deal stiller than any mouse if your father would tell a story you could understand, more particular if it was out of the Bible. Daniel and the Lions, or David and the Giant, or Peter in the Prison—these were the favorites then. Yes, and the history of Joseph and his brothers. Only you used to cry when his brothers put Joseph in the pit, and went home and told Jacob that wicked lie that almost broke the old man's heart."

"She's as fond of anything of that sort now as she was then," said Jacob Jones, pausing in his work; "or rather she's fonder than ever. I only wish we were able to give her a bit of schooling. It seems hard, for Mary is willing enough, and it's high time she was learning something. Why, Mrs. Evans, she can't read yet, because there's no one here to teach her."

Mary looked up, her face reddening, her eyes opening wide.

"Oh, if I only *could* learn!" she cried, eagerly. "It's so dreadful not to know how to read. If I could, I would read all those stories myself, and not trouble *anyone* to tell them!"

"You forget, Mary, we've no Bible," said Molly Jones, "and we can't afford to buy one either, so dear and scarce they are."

"Yes," replied Mrs. Evans, "it's a great need in our country of Wales. My husband was telling me only the other day that this shortage of Welsh Bibles is getting to be spoken of everywhere. Even those who can afford to pay for them find there are none available, as often as not. And *poor* people can't get them at all. But we hope a Society in London may print some more soon. It won't be before they're wanted, either!

"But with all this talk, Mrs. Jones," continued the farmer's wife, "I am forgetting my errand in coming here, and that was to ask if you'd any new-laid eggs. I've a large order sent me, and our hens are laying badly, so that I can't make up the number. I've been collecting a few here and there, but I haven't enough yet."

"Mary knows more about the hens and eggs than I do," said Molly, looking at her daughter, who had not put a stitch into her patch while the talk about Bibles had been going on, and whose cheeks and eyes showed in their deepened color how interested she had been in what had been said.

But now Mary jumped from her low seat, saying, "I'll get what we have, Mrs. Evans."

Presently she came in with a basket containing about a dozen eggs. The farmer's wife put them into her bag, paid for them, then rose to take her leave.

"And remember this, little maid," she said, kindly, when after saying goodbye to Jacob and Molly, she was at the door. "Remember this, my girl; as soon as you know how to read—if by that time you still have no Bible —you may come to the farm when you like, and read and study ours. That is, if you can manage to get so far!"

12

"It's only two miles, that's nothing!" said Mary, with a glance down at her strong bare feet. "I'd walk further than that for such a pleasure." "At least I would, if ever I *did* learn to read."

"Now, never mind! The likes of you wasn't made to sit in the dark always," replied Mrs. Evans in her cheery, comfortable tones. "If the Lord has made you want to read, He'll find the way, be very sure of that. Remember, Mary, when the crowds that went with Jesus were hungry, He did not send them away empty, though no one knew how they were to be fed. He'll take care you get the bread of life too, however unlikely it seems now. Goodbye, and God bless you, my child!" and Mrs. Evans, with a parting nod to the weaver and his wife, and another to Mary, went out. Quickly she got into her pony cart, which was waiting for her in the road, under the care of one of the farm boys.

Mary stood at the door and watched their visitor till she was out of sight. Then her thoughts formed themselves into a prayer something like this:

"Dear Lord, You gave bread to the hungry people in the old time, and You taught and blessed even the poorest. Please let me learn, and not grow up in darkness."

Then she shut the door and came and sat down, resolving in her heart that if God heard and answered her prayer, and she learned to read His Word, she would do what she could, all her life long, to help others as she herself had been helped.

CHAPTER 3

A Surprise

Two years passed since Mrs. Evans's visit, and still Mary's prayer seemed as far as ever from being answered. "Please let me learn, and not grow up in darkness."

With greater understanding and patience, Mary went about her daily duties. Her mother depended upon her for many things, and Mary had less time for dreaming now. Though Cader Idris was still the spot with which her imagination associated Bible scenes and pictures, she had little time to spare for anything but her everyday duties.

Mary still went with her mother to the midweek meetings at the chapel. From coming into contact with older people, rather than with children of her own age, she would have been called an old-fashioned girl if she had lived in a place where any difference was known between old fashions and new!

One evening Jacob Jones came home from Abergynolwyn, a village two miles away from

Llanfihangel. He had been selling the woollen cloth which he and Molly had been making during the past months.

Jacob had been away most of the day, yet he did not seem tired. His eyes were bright, and his lips wore a smile as he entered the cottage and sat down in his accustomed place in the chimney corner.

Mary, whose observant eye was sure to note the slightest change in her father's face and manner, sprang up and stood before him, regarding his bright face searchingly.

"What is it, father?" she asked, her own dark eyes flashing back the light in his. "Something pleasant has happened, or you wouldn't look like that!"

"What a sharp little daughter it is!" replied Jacob, drawing Mary nearer and seating her upon his knee. "What a very sharp little girl to find out that her old dad has something to tell!"

"And is it something that concerns me, father?" asked Mary.

"It is something that concerns you most of all, and us through you."

"What can it be?" murmured Mary, with a quick, impatient little sigh.

"Yes, what is it?" asked Mrs. Jones, sounding quite impatient herself. "We both want to know!"

"Well," replied Jacob, "what would you say, Molly dear, to our daughter here becoming quite a scholar; perhaps knowing how to read and write, and all a deal better than her parents ever did before her?"

"Oh, father!"

The exclamation came from Mary, who in her

excitement had slipped from Jacob's knee, and now stood facing him, breathless with suspense, her hands closely clasped. Jacob looked at her a moment without speaking; then he said,

"Yes, my girl, there is a *school* to be opened at Abergynolwyn, and a master is chosen already. And as you think nought of a two miles' walk, you shall go and learn all you can."

"Oh, father!"

"Well," rejoined Jacob, now laughing outright, "how many 'Oh fathers!' are we going to have? But I thought you'd be glad, my girl, and I was not wrong. You are pleased, aren't you?"

There was a pause; then Mary's reply came low spoken, but with such deep feeling in its tones.

"Pleased, father? Yes, indeed, for now I shall learn to *read the Bible.*"

Then a thought struck her, and a shadow came across the happy face as she said,

"But, mother, perhaps you won't be able to spare me?"

"Spare you? Yes I will, child, though I can't deny as how it will be difficult for me to do without you as my right hand and help. But for your good, my girl, I would do harder things than that."

"Dear, good mother!" cried Mary, putting an arm about Molly's neck and kissing her. "But I don't want you to work too hard and tire yourself. I'll get up an hour or two earlier, and do all I can before I start for school."

Then as the excited girl sat down again to her work, her heart, in its joyfulness, sent up a song of thanksgiving to the Lord who had heard her prayer, and was now opening the way for her to learn, that she might not grow up in darkness.

Presently Jacob spoke. "I went to see the room where the school is to be held, and who should come in while I was there but Mr. Charles of Bala. I'd often heard of him before, but I'd never seen him, and I was glad to set eyes on him for once."

"What does he look like, Jacob?" asked Molly.

'Well Molly, I never was a very good one for describing faces, but I should say he was between forty and fifty years old, with a fine big forehead which doesn't look as though it had unfurnished apartments to let behind it, but quite the opposite, as though he had done, a sight of thinking, and meant to do a great deal more. Still his face isn't anything so *very* special till he smiles. Then it's like sunshine, and goes to your heart, and warms you right through. Now I've seen him, and heard him speak, I can understand how he does so much good. I hear he's going about from place to place opening schools for the poor children, who would grow up ignorant otherwise."

"Like me!" murmured Mary, under her breath.

"And who's the master that's to be set over the school at Abergynolwyn?" asked Molly.

"I heard tell that his name is John Ellis," replied Jacob. "A good man, and right for the work, so they say; and I hope it'll prove so."

"And how soon is the school to open, Jacob?" asked Molly.

"In about three weeks, I believe," answered Jacob. "And now, Mary my girl, if you can bring yourself to think of such a thing as supper, after what I've been

The Rev. Thomas Charles of Bala.
(From the painting in the Bible House)

telling you, suppose you get some ready, for I haven't eaten since noon."

The following three weeks passed more slowly for Mary Jones than any three *months* she could remember before! The long wait showed itself in impatience. Her home duties at this time were not done so cheerfully or so quickly as usual, for her thoughts were far away, her heart being set on the thing she had longed for so much.

"If *this* is the way it's going to be, Jacob," said Molly to her husband one evening, "I shall wish there had never been a thought of school at Abergynolwyn. The girl's so off her head that she goes about like someone in a dream. What will it be like when that school begins? I daren't think!"

"Don't you fret," replied Jacob smiling. "It'll all come right. Don't you see that her busy brain has been longing to grow, and now that there's a chance of some learning, she's all in a state. But you'll find, when she once gets started, she'll go on all right with her duties at home. She's but ten years old, Molly, after all, and for my own part I'm not so sorry to see there's a bit of the child left in her, even if it shows itself this way."

This longest three weeks that Mary ever spent came to an end at last, and she began to go to school, taking a very important step forward.

What other children called hard work was to Mary only pleasure, and her eagerness was so great that she was almost always at the top of her class. In an incredibly short time she began to read and write.

John Ellis, the master, had a quick eye for seeing the character and talents of his pupils. He encouraged Mary in the school; and the girl repaid the master's kindness by working hard and willingly.

Molly Jones could find no fault now with Mary's performance of her home duties. She rose early, and did her work before breakfast; and after her return from school in the afternoon she again helped in the home, only keeping for herself time enough to prepare her school lessons for the next day.

At school she was well liked, and never seemed to be regarded with jealousy by her companions, because of the kind way in which she was willing to help others whenever she could.

One morning a small girl was crying sadly when she reached school. On being questioned as to what was the matter, she said that on the way a big dog had snatched at the paper bag in which she was bringing her dinner. The dog had carried it off, and so she would be hungry all day.

Some of the children laughed at the girl for her carelessness, and called her a coward for not running after the dog and getting back her dinner!

But Mary whispered something in the girl's ear, dried the wet eyes, and presently the child was smiling and happy again.

When dinner time came, Mary and the dinnerless child sat close together in a corner, and more than half of Mary's provisions found their way to the smaller child.

The other scholars looked on, apparently feeling ashamed that none but Mary Jones had thought of doing so kind and neighborly an action, at the cost of a little self denial. But the lesson was not lost upon them, and often Mary's influence made itself felt in the school for good.

On another occasion Mary was just getting ready to set off on her two miles' journey home, when she spied in a corner of the now deserted schoolroom a young boy with a book open before him, and a smeared slate and blunt pencil by his side. Tears were falling over his unfinished task and evidently he was in the last stages of despair. He had dawdled away his time during the school hours, and had not listened when the lesson had been explained, and now the strict school discipline required that he should stay behind when the rest had gone, and attend to the work which he had left unfinished.

Mary had a headache that day, and was longing to get home. But the sight of that tearful face in the corner banished all thoughts of herself, and as the voices of the other children died away in the distance, she crossed the room, and leaned over the boy's shoulder.

"What is it, Robbie? Oh, I see, you've got to do that sum. I mayn't do it for you, you know, because that would be a sort of cheating, but I can tell you how to do it yourself, and I think I can make it plain."

So saying, Mary fetched a little bit of wet rag, and washed the slate, and then got an old knife and sharpened the pencil.

"Now," said she, smiling cheerily, "see I'll put down the sum as it is in the book." Then she wrote on the slate in clear, if not very elegant figures, the sum in question.

Encouraged now, Robbie gave his mind to his task, and with a little help it was soon done; and Mary with a light heart, which made up for her heavy head, set off home, very glad that what she was herself learning could be a help to others.

Not long after the start of the day school, a Sunday

school also was opened. The very first Sunday that children were taught there, Mary appeared as clean and fresh as soap and water could make her. Bright eyes and an eager face showed the keen interest she felt, and her deep wish to learn.

That Sunday evening, after service in the chapel, as Mrs. Evans, the farmer's wife, was just going to get into her pony cart to drive home, she felt a light touch on her arm, while a young voice she knew said, "Please, may I speak to you a moment?"

"Surely, my child," replied the woman, turning her smiling friendly face to Mary. "What have you got to say to me?"

"Two years ago, please, you were so kind as to promise that when I'd learned to read I should come to the farm and read your Bible."

"I did, I remember it well," answered Mrs. Evans. "Well, child, do you now know how to read?"

"Yes, I do," responded Mary. "And I've joined the Sunday school, so there are Bible lessons to prepare. And be so kind as to let me come up to the farm one day in the week—perhaps Saturday, when I've a half-holiday —I could never thank you enough."

"There's no need for thanks. Come, and welcome! I shall expect you next Saturday and may the Lord make His Word a great blessing to you!"

Mrs. Evans held Mary's hand one moment, then she got into her cart, and the pony started off quickly towards home, as though he knew that old Farmer Evans was laid up with rheumatism, and that his wife wished to get back to him as soon as possible!

CHAPTER 4

Two Miles to a Bible

Mr. Evans's farm was a curious old-fashioned place. The house was a large rambling building, with many odd ups and downs, and windows in all sorts of unexpected places. And yet there was a homely comfort, not always to be found in far finer and more imposing houses. At the back were the out-buildings—the sheds and cow houses, the poultry pen, the stables and pigsties. Stretching away beyond these again were the home paddock, the drying-ground, and a small enclosed field, which went by the name of Hospital Meadow, because it was used for sick animals that needed a rest.

It was the farmer, Mr. Evans, who had spoken so kindly to Mary two years earlier at the meeting. He was still the same good, honest, industrious, God-fearing man, never forgetting in his work what he owed to the Giver of all, who sends His rain for the watering of the seed, and His sun for the ripening of the harvest.

Nor did he find fault with God if the rain came down upon the hay before it was safely stored, or if an early autumn gale laid his wheat level with the earth from which it sprang, before the sickle could be put into it for harvest. Nor did he complain and grumble even when disease showed itself among the cattle and sheep of which he was justly proud. In short, he was contented with what the Lord sent and with what the Lord allowed.

Mr. and Mrs. Evans had three children. The eldest was already grown up and a great comfort and help to her mother. The younger children were boys, who went to a grammar school in a town a mile or two away.

Mary was welcomed into the family with love and kindness. But she was shy and timid the first time, for the farmhouse was a much finer place than any home she had previously seen. Yet there was an atmosphere of warmth, and there were signs of plenty, which were unknown in Jacob Jones's poor cottage, where there was nothing more than the barest of essentials.

But Mary's shyness did not last long. Indeed it disappeared soon after she had crossed the threshold, where she was met by Mrs. Evans.

Mary had put on the best clothes she could find for this important visit. Carefully she had trimmed the sleeves and collar with small pieces of old lace, making the most of the few items of well worn clothing she possessed.

"Come in, my girl," Mrs. Evans said, drawing Mary into the cozy old-fashioned kitchen, where a kettle was singing on the hob. The low-ceilinged room was filled with an enticing fragrance of currant shortcake, baking for an early tea.

"There, get warm, dear," continued Mrs. Evans, "and then you shall go to the parlor, and look in the Bible.

And have you got a pencil and some paper to take notes if you want them?"

"Yes, thank you. I brought them with me," replied Mary.

For a few minutes she sat there, basking in the pleasant cheery glow of the firelight. Then she was shown to the parlor, where, on the table in the center of the room, was the precious book covered with a clean white cloth. The white cloth was not a sign that the Bible was never used. On the contrary, it was always read at prayers night and morning; for the family loved to study God's Word, and seek to understand its teachings.

"There's no need to tell you to be careful of our Bible, and to turn over the pages gently, Mary, I'm sure," said Mrs. Evans. "You would do that anyway, I know. And now, I'll leave you and the Bible together. When you've learned your lesson for Sunday school, and read all you want, come back into the kitchen and have some tea before you go."

Then the farmer's wife went away, leaving Mary alone with a Bible for the first time in her life.

It was several minutes before she could bring herself to raise the white cloth. At last folding it neatly, Mary laid it on one side.

Then, with trembling hands, she opened the book; opened it at the fifth chapter of John, and her eyes caught these words, "Chwiliwch yr ysgrythurau; canys ynddynt hwynt yr ydych chwi yn meddwl cael bywyd tragwyddol: a hwynt-hwy yw y rhai sydd yn tystiolaethu am danaf fi." ("You study the Scriptures, because you

Chained Bibles, owned by the church
and kept there for people to read.

think that in them you will find eternal life. And these very Scriptures speak about Me!" John 5:39).

"I will, I will!" she cried, sensing that although the words had first been spoken by Jesus to people who would not accept Him, they were now being spoken directly to her by her Heavenly Father, in His love. "I *will* search *and* learn all I can. Oh, if I had a Bible of my own!"

And this wish, this prayer for the rare and coveted treasure, was the first note which, years after, spread in volume, until it rolled in waves of sound over the whole earth. The longing in a young girl's heart was destined to be a means of light and knowledge to millions of souls in the future.

To Mary this was just a private happening in her life, but God was planning to carry out His great will. In a Welsh farmhouse, with all the people there quite unaware of the fact, Mary Jones was being prepared by God to begin a work whose importance is not to be calculated on this side of eternity.

When Mary had finished studying the Bible lesson for Sunday, and had enjoyed a good meal in the cosy kitchen, she said goodbye to her friends, and set off home. Her mind was full of the one great longing, out of which a resolution was slowly shaping itself.

And then it was formed at last!

"*I will* have a Bible of my own!" she said aloud, surprising herself with the loudness of her voice. "I must have one, if I save up for it for ten years!" And by the time this plan had been settled in her mind Mary reached her home.

Christmas came, and with it some holidays for Mary and the other scholars who attended the school at Abergynolwyn. Mary would have been sorry that lessons stopped, had it not been that during the holidays she had determined to carry out her plan for earning something towards buying her Bible.

Without neglecting her home duties, Mary managed to take on work for neighbors. Many were glad to give her a small sum of money. Now it was to mind a baby while the mother was at the washtub. Now to pick up sticks and brushwood in the woods for fuel; or to help to mend and patch the garments of the family for a weary mother, who was thankful to give a small sum for this welcome help.

And every halfpenny, every farthing, was put into a special moneybox which Jacob made for Mary. The box was kept in a cupboard, on a shelf where Mary could reach it, and it was a real and heartfelt joy to her when she could bring her day's earnings—the smallest copper coins, perhaps—and drop them in, longing for the time to come when they would have swelled to the required sum—a very large sum unfortunately—for buying a Bible.

Then one day, Mrs. Evans, knowing Mary's great wish, and wanting to encourage and help her, made her the present of a fine cockerel and two hens.

"No, no, my dear, don't thank me," said she, when Mary was trying to tell her how grateful she was. "I've done it, first to help you along with that Bible you've set your heart on, and then, too because I love you, and like to give you pleasure. So now, my child, when the hens begin to lay, which will be early in the spring, you can sell your eggs, for these will be your very own to do what you like with, and you can put the money to any use you please. And I think I know what you'll do with it," added Mrs. Evans, with a smile.

It happened that the first *silver* coin that Mary had the satisfaction of dropping into her box was earned before she had any eggs to sell. It came in quite a different way from the sums which she had so far received. She was walking one evening along the road from Tywyn, where she had been sent on an errand for her father. Looking over at the mountains, her foot struck against an object lying in the road. Stooping to pick it up, she found it was a large leather purse. Wondering whose it could be, Mary went on until, while still within half a mile of home, she met a man walking slowly, and evidently searching for something. He looked up as Mary approached, and she recognized him as Farmer Greaves, a brother-in-law of Mrs. Evans.

"Ah, good evening, Mary Jones," he said. "I've had such a loss! Coming home from market I dropped my purse, and—"

" *I've* just found a purse!" said Mary. "Is this it?"

"You've found a purse?" exclaimed the farmer eagerly. "Yes indeed, my dear, that is mine, and I'm very much obliged to you. No, stay a moment," he called after her, for Mary was already trudging off again. "I should like to give you a trifle for your hon—I mean just some trifle by way of thanks."

As he spoke, his finger and thumb closed on a bright shilling, which surely would not have been too much to give to a poor child who had found a heavy purse. But he thought better (or worse) of it, and took out instead a small silver sixpence and handed it to Mary, who took it with very heartfelt thanks, and ran home as quickly as possible to drop her treasure safely into the box, where it was destined to keep its poorer copper brethren company for many a long year.

The Christmas holidays were soon over, and then it was difficult for Mary to keep up with her daily lessons *and* her Sunday school study. The latter meant weekly visits to the farmhouse for reading the Bible. What with these and her home duties, sometimes weeks passed without Mary having time to earn a penny towards the purchase of the Bible.

Sometimes, too, she was rather late in reaching home on the Saturday evenings, and now and again Molly was uneasy about her. For Mary *would* come by short cuts over the hills, along ways which, however safe in the daytime, were rough and unpleasant, if not dangerous, after dark. In these long winter evenings the daylight vanished very early.

It was on one of these occasions that Molly and Jacob Jones were sitting and waiting for their daughter.

The old clock had already struck eight. Mary had never been so late as this before.

"Our Mary ought to be home, Jacob," said Molly, breaking a silence disturbed only by the noise of Jacob's busy loom. "It's got as dark as dark, and there's no moon tonight. The way's a rugged one if she comes the short cut across the hill—and she's not one to choose a long road if she can find a shorter, bless her! She's more than after her time. I hope no harm's come to her," and Molly walked to the window and looked out.

"Don't be fretting yourself, Molly," replied Jacob,

pausing in his work. "Mary's out on a good errand, and He who put the love of good things in her heart will take care of her."

Jacob spoke solemnly, but with a tone of conviction that comforted his wife, as words of his had often done before. Just then a light step bounded up to the door, the latch was lifted, and Mary's young figure entered the cottage, her dark eyes shining, her cheeks flushed, a look of eager animation overspreading the whole of her bright face and seeming to diffuse a radiance round the cottage, while it shone reflected in the faces of Jacob and Molly.

"Well, child, what have you learned today?" questioned Jacob. "Have you studied your lesson for the Sunday school?"

"Ay, father, that I have, and a beautiful lesson it was," responded Mary. "It was the lesson, and Mr. Evans together, that kept me so late."

"How so, Mary?" asked Molly. "We've been right down uneasy about you, fearing lest something had happened to you."

"You needn't have been so, mother," replied Mary, with something of her father's quiet assurance. "God knew what I was about, and He would not let any harm come to me. Oh, father, the more I read about Him the more I want to know, and I shall never rest until I've a Bible of my own. But today I've brought home a big bit of the farmer's Bible with me!"

"What do you mean, Mary? How could you do such a thing?" asked her mother in amazement.

"Only in my head of course!" replied Mary, laughing. Then she added, "And in my heart."

"And what is the bit?" asked Jacob.

"It's the seventh chapter of Matthew," said Mary. "Our Sunday lesson was from the first verse to the end of the twelfth verse. But it was so easy and so beautiful, that I went on and on, till I'd learned the whole chapter. And just as I had finished, Mr. Evans came in and asked me if I understood it all. And when I said there were some bits that puzzled me, he was so kind and explained them. If you like, I'll repeat the chapter for you."

So Jacob pushed away his work and took his old seat in the chimney corner, and Molly began some knitting, while Mary sat down on a stool at her father's feet. Then beginning at the first verse, she repeated the whole chapter without a single mistake, without a moment's hesitation, and with a tone and emphasis, which showed her love and understanding of the words she had learnt.

"Mark my words," said Jacob that night, when Mary had gone to bed, "that child will do a work for the Lord before she dies. Do you not see how He Himself is leading and guiding His lamb into green pastures and beside still waters? Why Molly, when she repeated that verse, 'Ask, and you will receive', I saw her eyes shine, and her cheeks aglow again, and I knew she was thinking of the Bible that she's set her heart on. I doubt not she's praying for that Bible often enough when we know nothing about it. And the Lord will give it to her someday. Of that I'm certain. Yes, Molly, our Mary will have her Bible!"

"Gofynwch, a rhoddir i chwi; ceisiwch, a chwi a gewch; curwch, ac fe agorir i chwi. Canys pob un sydd yn gofyn, sydd yn derbyn; a'r neb sydd yn ceisio, sydd yn cael; ac i'r hwn sydd yn curo, yr agorir."

("Ask, and you will receive; seek, and you will find; knock, and the door will be opened to you. For everyone who asks will receive, and anyone who seeks will find, and the door will be opened to him who knocks" Matthew 7:7-8).

CHAPTER 5

The Mysterious Teacher

While Mary was being taught by John Ellis, she was also being prepared by God for a part in His plan for bringing the Bible to people all around the world.

At the same time, a young man called Lewis Williams, from Pennal, was also learning to read and write. His parents had been too poor to manage any sort of education for him. As he grew up, he was a reckless and wild youth, a trouble to his neighbors, and completely unaware of God and His love. Yet God had a plan for him, too.

These are the words that changed his life:

"Eithr y mae Duw yn canmol ei gariad tu ag attom; o blegid a nyni etto yn bechaduriaid, i Grist farw trosom ni. Mwy ynte o lawer, a nyni yn awr wedi ein cyfiawnhau trwy ei waed ef, y'n hachubir rhag digofaint trwyddo ef."

"But God has shown us how much He loves us—it was while we were still sinners that Christ died for us! By His death we are now put right with God; how much more, then, will we be saved by Him from God's anger!" Romans 5:8-9.

When he was about eighteen years old, Lewis Williams chanced to be at a prayer meeting, when a Mr. Jones, of Mathafarn, was speaking on this fifth chapter of the Epistle to the Romans.

The word of God came to Lewis Williams in a fresh and striking manner. It was the means of carrying home to his heart the realization of sin. A change was seen in him from that time on. It gradually deepened until none could doubt that he had become a real and committed Christian.

While he was being admitted to membership in a little Methodist church at Cwmllinian, he was asked, "If Jesus Christ asked you to do some work for Him, would you do it?"

His answer gives the key to his success: "Oh yes; *whatever* Jesus required of me I would do *at once.*"

Some years after, when in a place called Trychiad, near Llanegryn, he noticed boys in the neighborhood who had no teaching. Filled with a longing to do some special work for his Heavenly Master, he made up his mind to establish a Sunday school, and a week-night school as well if possible, in order to teach the lads to read their Welsh language.

This would have been nothing remarkable if Lewis Williams had received any sort of education himself. But as he had never spent a day in school in his life, and could hardly read a word correctly, the thought of teaching others seemed, to say the least, rather a wild idea!

But the old saying has often been proved correct, that where there is a will there is a way; and so it was true in the experience of Lewis Williams.

Through the young man's hard work and courage, his school was opened in a short time, and he began the work teaching the Welsh alphabet to the lowest class by singing it to the tune of "The March of the Men of Harlech."

Dr. Moffat tried the same plan of melody lessons forty years later, with a number of children in Africa, teaching them their letters to the tune of "Auld Lang Syne" with great success.

But Lewis Williams could hardly restrict his teaching to the lowest class in the school. Yet in teaching the older boys he was coming face to face with an obstacle which might well have seemed too great to anyone with less courage and determination.

The master could not read, or at least he could not read well, yet he had taken on the work of teaching reading to the lads in his school!

Painfully aware of his lack of knowledge, before commencing his Sunday school work or his evening classes, he used to pay a visit to a woman called Betty Evans who had learned to read well. Under her tuition he prepared the lessons he was going to give that day or the next, so that in reality the master of that flourishing little school was only ahead of his scholars by a few hours!

At other times he would invite a number of boys from the local grammar school to come for reading and discussion. All this was, of course, in the Welsh language.

With quiet tact and careful planning he would arrange that the subject taken should include the lesson which he would shortly have to give.

While the reading and talk went on, he listened with the greatest attention. The discussions as to the meaning or pronunciation of the more difficult words was all that he wanted to find out from the grammar school boys.

But none of these boys had an inkling that the man who invited them, who questioned them so closely, and listened so attentively, was himself a learner, and relied on them for the proper construction of phrases, or for the correct pronunciation of words he would need for his next day's or next week's lessons!

His school days always started with prayer, and as the master had a restless unruly set of lads, he invented a somewhat odd way to get their attention.

Familiar with military drill through once being in the army, he would put the boys through a series of orders, and when they came to "stand at ease," and "attention!" he would at once, very briefly and simply, lead them in prayer!

While Lewis Williams was hard at work at Llanegryn, seeking to lead people to know Jesus and train minds to serve Him, it happened that Mr. Charles of Bala arrived at Bryncrug. He was intending to lead a meeting to be held at Abergynolwyn, and spent the night at the house of John Jones, the schoolmaster there.

Mr. Charles asked Mr. Jones if he knew of a suitable person to take charge of one of his recently established schools in the neighbourhood.

John Jones replied that he had heard of a young man at Llanegryn, who taught the children both on week-nights and Sundays.

"But," added the schoolmaster, "as I hear that he himself cannot read, I can hardly understand how he is able to teach others."

"Impossible!" exclaimed Mr. Charles. "How can anyone teach what he does not himself know?"

"Still, they say that he does," replied John Jones.

Mr. Charles asked to see this mysterious instructor of youth, who was reported as passing on to others what he did not himself possess! The next day, accordingly, summoned by John Jones, the young schoomaster made his appearance. His old clothes and his rough country manner showed that he was anything but a man of learning.

"Well, my young friend," said Mr. Charles, in the pleasant way that was natural to him, "they tell me you keep a school at Llanegryn yonder, on Sundays and week-nights, to teach children to read. Have you many scholars?"

"Yes, sir, far more than I am able to teach," replied Lewis Williams.

"And do they learn a little by your teaching?" asked Mr. Charles, as kindly as ever, but with a slight hint of disbelief.

"I think some of them learn, sir," responded the young teacher, very quietly. A sense of his own feeling of being unequal to the task showed itself painfully both in his voice and manner.

"It is plain that you only speak Welsh. But do you understand *any* English?" questioned Mr. Charles.

"Only a stray word or two, sir, which I picked up when serving in the army."

"Do you read Welsh fluently?"

41

Llan-y-cil Church
(The burial place of the Rev. Thomas Charles)

"No, sir, I can read but little, but I am doing my very best to learn."

"Were you at a school before beginning to teach?" asked Mr. Charles, more and more interested in the young man who stood before him.

"No, sir. I never had a day's schooling in my life."

"And your parents did not teach you to read while you were at home?"

"No, sir, my parents could not read a word for themselves."

Mr. Charles opened his Welsh Bible at the first chapter of the Epistle to the Hebrews, and asked Lewis Williams to read a few verses.

"Duw, wedi iddo lafaru lawer gwaith, a llawer modd, gynt wrth y tadau trwy'r prophwydi, yn y dyddiau diweddaf hyn a lafarodd wrthym ni yn ei Fab."

("In the past, God spoke to our ancestors many times and in many ways through the prophets" Hebrews 1:1).

Slowly, hesitatingly, and with several mistakes, the young man stumbled with difficulty through the first verse.

"That will do, my lad," said Mr. Charles. "Just how you are able to teach others to read, passes my understanding. Tell me now, by what plan you instruct the children."

Then the young teacher gave an account of his musical ABC; the lessons given to himself by Betty Evans; the readings and discussions of the grammar school boys; and the scholars playing at "soldiers".

As Lewis Williams proceeded with his confessions (for such they appeared to be to him), Mr. Charles carefully and gently penetrated through the roughness of the teacher to the real force of character of the man. He saw that this follower of Jesus had worked hard to improve his one talent, and work with it in the Master's service, and that he only needed help to become a most valuable servant of Christ. So he recommended him to place himself for a time under the tuition of John Jones, to become a more effective school teacher.

During the following three months, Lewis Williams followed the advice of Mr. Charles; and this was all the schooling that he ever had.

Every hour Lewis Williams could spare was devoted to study, in order to fit himself for one of the schoolmasters' places that were under Mr. Charles special control and management. He used to visit neighboring churches, to study the preaching of the ministers there. At last, in the year 1799—that is, when he was about twenty-five years of age—he was engaged by Mr. Charles as a paid teacher in one of his schools. He moved to Abergynolwyn a year later, and here, among his pupils, was young Mary Jones.

In later years, he established many new schools and revived others. At length he became a preacher, so great was his ambition in his Master's service, and so anxious was he that all should know the truth and join in the work of the Lord.

And so we return to Mary Jones, who was nearly sixteen years old at the time Lewis Williams became the schoolmaster at Abergynolwyn.

She was as full of life and energy as ever. Nor had her enthusiasm faltered for one moment over her plan for the purchase of a Bible. Through six long years she had hoarded every penny, denying herself the little luxuries which the poverty of her life made so attractive to one so young. She continued her visits to the farmhouse, and while she studied her Bible lessons for Sunday school, so her desire to possess God's Holy Book for herself grew greater rather than less.

What joy it would be, she often thought, if every day she could read and learn by heart passages of Scripture, filling her mind and heart with God's teaching.

"But the time *will* come," she added, "when I shall have my Bible. Yes, though I have waited so long, the time *will* come." Then on her knees beside her bed she prayed aloud, "Dear Lord, let the time come quickly!"

Mary was more useful, more her mother's right hand, than ever. And her father, as he looked into her clear, honest, intelligent dark eyes, and heard her recite her lesson for school, or tell him all the teaching to which she had that day listened, thanked the Lord in his heart for his daughter. Often he prayed that she might grow up to be a blessing to all she would meet in the future.

CHAPTER 6

On the Way

"Mother! Father! Mrs. Evans has just paid me for that work I did for her, and it is more than I expected. Now I have enough to buy a Bible. I'm so happy I don't know what to do!"

Mary had just come from the Evans' farmhouse, and as she bounded into Ty'nyddol with the joyful news, Jacob stopped his loom and held out both hands.

"Is it really so, Mary? After six years' saving! Nay then, God be thanked, who first put the wish into your heart, and then gave you patience to wait and work to get the thing you wanted. Bless you, my child!" And Jacob laid a hand upon his daughter's head.

"But tell me, father," said Mary after a little pause, "*where* am I to buy the Bible? There are no Bibles to be had here, *or* at Abergynolwyn."

"I cannot tell you, Mary, but our preacher, William Huw, will know," replied Jacob. "You will do well to go to him tomorrow, and ask how you're to get the book."

Acting on her father's suggestion, Mary went the next day to Llechwedd to William Huw, and asked the question so all-important to her. But he replied that no copy could be obtained locally. He knew of no place nearer than Bala. Then he added that he feared lest all the Bibles received there by Mr. Charles from London had been sold or promised months ago.

This was discouraging news, and Mary went home, cast down, but not in despair. There was still, she reflected, a chance that *one* copy of the Bible remained in Mr. Charles' possession; and if so, it would be hers!

The long distance—over twenty-five miles—the unknown road, the far-famed, but to her, strange minister —all this, if it a little frightened her, did not for one moment change her mind. She *would* have the Bible she had saved for all these years!

At first, Jacob and Molly objected to Mary walking all the way to Bala. They would not be able to go with her for the journey was very difficult.

Then Jacob relented. "If it is the Lord's will that she has her Bible," he said to Molly, "then He will keep her and lead her safely over the mountains. It would be wrong of us to try and go against His will."

So Mary had her way, and having received permission for her long journey, she went to a neighbor living near. Telling her of her proposed expedition, Mary asked if she would lend her a bag to carry home the treasure on her shoulder should she obtain it.

The neighbor, thinking of Mary's many acts of thoughtful kindness towards herself and her children, and glad to be able to show her thanks, put the bag into the girl's hand, and bade her goodbye with a hearty "God speed you!"

The next morning, a fresh, breezy day in spring, in the year 1800, Mary rose almost as soon as it was light.

She washed and dressed with unusual care; for this was to be a day of days—the day for which she had waited for years, and which must, she thought, make her the happiest of girls—*or* bring to her such grief and disappointment as she had never yet known.

Her one pair of shoes—far too precious a possession to be worn on a twenty-five mile walk—Mary placed in the bag, intending to put them on as soon as she reached the town of Bala.

Early as was the hour, Molly and Jacob were both up to give Mary her breakfast of hot milk and bread, and have family prayers, asking specially for God's blessing on their daughter's undertaking, and for His protection and care during her journey.

This helped and encouraged Mary, and after kissing her parents, she went out into the dawn of that lovely day—a day which she remembered clearly till the last hour of her life.

She set out at a good pace—not too quick, for that would have wearied her before even a quarter of her journey could be done. With an even, steady walk, her bare brown feet treading lightly but firmly along the road, her head held high, her clear eyes glistening, she went— the happiest girl on that spring morning in all the country round! Never before had everything about her looked to Mary as it looked on that memorable morning.

The old mountain seemed to gaze down protectingly upon her. The very sun, as it came up on the eastern horizon, appeared to have a smile specially for Mary.

Bala Lake

The larks soared from the meadow till their trilling died away in the sky, like a tuneful prayer sent up to God. The rabbits looked out at her from leafy nooks and holes, and even a squirrel, as it ran up a tree, stopped to glance, as much as to say, "Good morning, Mary; have a good journey!" And the girl's heart was attuned to the loveliness of nature, full of thankfulness for the past and of hope for the future.

To Mary, Thomas Charles was as yet no more than a name. To those who knew him, he was a mighty man of God.

Thomas Charles of Bala. By many he was called the "Apostolic Charles of Bala". Like the Apostles in the early Christian Church, he went from place to place, teaching the love and forgiveness of the Lord. As he went, he started schools. Here adults and children could come and learn of God, and of His Son Jesus who wanted them for His own.

At the age of eighteen Thomas Charles had given himself to Jesus and his first work for the Lord was in his own home. Here he began family worship, and had an influence as powerful as it was loving and gentle.

His education was begun at Carmarthen, and continued at Oxford. The Rev. John Newton was a good friend to him during a part of his student life. On one occasion his holidays were spent at the house of this excellent man.

The Rev. Thomas Charles became an ordained minister in the Church of England in due course. But owing to the faithful and outspoken style of his preaching, many of his own denomination in those days took offence and would not accept him. So he left the Church of England and joined one of the Welsh Methodist churches. His greatest work, so people said, was the establishment of Day and Sunday Schools in Wales. The organization of these, the selection of paid teachers, visiting the various schools, made Mr. Charles' life a very busy one. But he could see that his hard work was not in vain. Wherever he went he was carrying the Good News, and proving it in his life, in the service of Jesus. The darkness that hung over the people lifted, and the true light began to shine.

Such was the man, and such his work up to the time of Mary's journey. Great though this work was, God had even greater plans for him. But he still had some hours left before God would present him with a challenge he would be unable to refuse—for Mary Jones was not yet halfway to Bala!

About the middle of the day Mary stopped to rest, and to eat some of the food which her mother had provided for her. Under a tree in a grassy hollow not far from the road, she half reclined, protected from the sun by the tender green of the spring foliage. Then she began cooling her hot dusty feet in the soft damp grass that spread like a velvet carpet all over the hollow.

Before long Mary spied a little stream, trickling down a hill on its way to the sea, and here she drank, and washed her face and hands and feet, and was refreshed.

Half an hour's quiet rested her thoroughly. Soon she jumped up, slung the bag over her shoulder again, and recommenced her journey.

The rest of the way, along a dusty road for the most part, and under the warm sun, was now tiring. Mary plodded on, though her feet were blistered and cut with the stones, and her head ached and limbs were very weary.

A kind cottager, as she passed, gave her a drink of butter-milk, and a farmer's young daughter, as Mary neared Bala, offered her a share of the supper she was eating as she sat in the porch in the cool of the evening. But Mary could remember nothing more of her journey till she finally got to Bala.

On arriving there she put on her shoes, and followed the instructions that had been given to her by William Huw, and went to the house of David Edwards an elderly and much respected Methodist preacher at Bala.

He received her most kindly, questioned her as to why she had travelled far, but ended by telling her that it was now too late in the day to see Mr. Charles.

"But," added the old preacher, seeing his young visitor's disappointment, "you must sleep here tonight, and we will go to Mr. Charles as soon as I see a light in his study window tomorrow morning, so that you may see to your errand in good time, and be able to return home before night."

With grateful thanks Mary accepted the hospitality offered her, and after a simple supper she was shown into the little attic room where she was to sleep.

There, after saying by memory a favorite chapter of the Bible, and speaking with God in prayer, Mary lay down, her mind and body alike resting. Her faith made her sure that her journey would not be in vain, for He

Bala

who had led her safely this far would surely give her her heart's desire.

And the curtains of night fell softly around the preacher's humble dwelling. The sleep of those within was sweet, and their safety assured. For, watching over them was the God of the night and the day—the God whom they loved and trusted, and underneath them were the Everlasting Arms.

CHAPTER 7

Tears

Bala is still a quiet little town, situated near the end of Bala Lake, on the north side of a wide, cultivated valley. When Mary Jones walked there for her Bible, it was more quiet and rural still.

Around the town, mountains rise to look down upon the large lake. In the town itself, the road is straight and level as it runs past the rugged but often attractive cottages and houses. All was quiet this night, and Mary did not wake until David Edwards, the old preacher, knocked at her door at early dawning.

"Wake up, Mary Jones! Mr. Charles is an early riser, and will soon be at work. The dawn is breaking; get up!"

Mary started up, rubbing her eyes. The time had really come, then, and in a few minutes she would know what was to be the result of her long waiting.

Her heart beat quicker as she washed and dressed, but her excitement calmed when she sat down for a minute or two on the side of her bed, and thought of the 23rd Psalm.

"Yr Arglwydd *yw* fy Mugail; ni bydd eisiau arnaf." ("The Lord is my shepherd; I have everything I need" Psalm 23:1).

Mary felt as though she was of a truth being watched over and cared for by a loving Shepherd, and being led by Him.

Mary was soon ready, and she and David Edwards proceeded to Mr. Charles' house without having any breakfast.

"There's a light in his study," said the old preacher. "Our apostle is at his desk already. There are not many like him, Mary; always at work for the Master. The world would be better had we more."

Mary did not reply, but she listened intently as David Edwards knocked at the door. There was no answer, only the tread of shoes across the floor. The next moment the door opened, and Mr. Charles himself stood before them.

"Good morning, friend Edwards! And what brings you here so early? Come in, do," said the genial, hearty voice, which so many knew, and had cause to love. Then, as David Edwards entered, Mr. Charles noticed the figure behind him in the doorway.

A rather timid shrinking figure it was now, for Mary's courage was fast ebbing away, and she felt shy and frightened.

A few words of explanation passed between the old preacher and Mr. Charles. Then Mary was invited to enter the study.

Mr. Charles' house at Bala

"Now, my child," said Mr. Charles, "don't be afraid, but tell me all about yourself, where you live, and what your name is, and what you want."

At this Mary took courage and answered all Mr. Charles' questions, her voice (which at first was low and trembling) strengthening as her confidence returned. She told him all about her home and her parents, and her longing when quite a child for a Bible of her own. Then she told of the long years during which she had saved up her small earnings towards the purchase of a Bible— the sum being now complete.

Then Mr. Charles asked questions as to her Bible knowledge, and was delighted with the girl's replies, which showed how thoroughly she had studied the Book she loved so well.

"But how, my child," he asked in his gentle voice, "did you get to know the Bible as you do, when you do not own one for yourself?"

Then Mary told him of the visits to the farmhouse, and how, through the kindness of Farmer Evans and his wife, she had been able to study her Sunday school lessons and commit portions of the Bible to memory.

As Mary informed Mr. Charles of all that had taken place, he began to realize how brave, and patient, and earnest, and hopeful she had been through all these years of waiting. But when he learned how far Mary had now come to obtain possession of the coveted treasure, his bright face became overshadowed, and, turning to David Edwards, he said, sadly,

"I am indeed grieved that this dear girl should have come all the way from Llanfihangel to buy a Bible, because I am unable to supply her with one. The Welsh

Bibles that I received from London last year were all sold out months ago, except for a few copies which I have kept for friends whom I must not disappoint. Unfortunately the Society which has supplied Wales with the Scriptures will not print any more, and where to get Welsh Bibles to satisfy our country's need I do not know."

Until now, Mary had been looking up into Mr. Charles's face, with her great dark eyes full of hope and confidence. But as he spoke these words to David Edwards, and she noticed his overclouded face, and began to understand the full meaning of his words, the room seemed to her to darken suddenly.

Dropping into the nearest seat, Mary buried her face in her hands, and sobbed as, perhaps, few girls of her age had ever sobbed before.

It was all over, then, she said to herself—all of no use— the prayers, the longing, the waiting, the working, the saving for six long years, the weary walk with bare feet, the near prospect of her hopes being fulfilled, all, all in vain!

To a mind so filled with Bible verses as hers, the language of the Psalmist seemed the natural outburst for so great a grief.

"A anghofiodd Duw drugarhau? a gauodd efe ei drugareddau mewn sorriant?" ("Has God forgotten to be merciful? Has anger taken the place of His compassion?" Psalm 77:9).

All in vain—all of no use! And the young head, lately held so high, drooped lower and lower, and the sunburnt hands, roughened by work and exposure, could not hide the great hot tears that rolled down, chasing each other over cheeks out of which the accustomed rosy tint had fled, and falling unheeded through her fingers. There were a few moments during which only Mary's sobs broke the silence. But those sobs had appealed to Mr. Charles' heart with a strength he was wholly unable to resist.

With his own voice broken and unsteady he said, as he rose from his seat and laid a hand on the drooping head of the girl before him:

"My dear child, I see you *must* have a Bible, difficult as it is for me to spare you one. It is impossible, yes, simply impossible, to refuse you."

In the sudden burst of feeling that followed these words, Mary could not speak. Instead, she glanced up with such a face of mingled rain and sunshine—such a rainbow smile—such a look of joy and thankfulness in her brimming eyes, that tears filled the eyes of both Mr. Charles and David Edwards.

Mr. Charles turned away for a moment to a bookcase that stood behind him, and opening it, he drew forth a Bible.

Then, laying a hand once more on Mary's head, with the other he placed the Bible in her grasp. Looking down into the earnest glistening eyes upturned to him, he said:

"If you, my dear girl, are glad to receive this Bible, truly glad am I to be able to give it to you. Read it carefully, study it, treasure up the sacred words in your memory, and live your life by obeying the Lord's teachings."

And then as Mary, quite overcome with delight and thankfulness, began once more to sob, but softly and with sweet happy tears, Mr. Charles turned to the old preacher, and said, huskily,

"David Edwards, is not such a sight as this enough to melt the hardest heart? A girl, so poor, so very intelligent, so familiar with the Word of God, compelled to walk all the distance from Llanfihangel to Bala—about fifty miles there and back—to get a Bible! From this day I can never rest, until I find some way of supplying our country of Wales which cries out for this Word of God!"

Half an hour later Mary Jones was back at David Edwards' house. Here she had her breakfast before setting off on the long homeward journey.

The day was somewhat cloudy, but Mary did not notice it. Her heart was full of sunshine. The wind blew strongly, but a great calm was in her soul. Her young face was so full of happiness that the folk she met on the way could not help but smile as she skipped happily on, her bare feet seeming hardly to press the ground, and her eyes shining with deep content. The bag containing her newly-found treasure was no longer slung across her back, but clasped tightly in her arms.

The sun rose and burst through the clouds, glorifying all the landscape. Onward went Mary, her heart, like the lark's song, full of thanksgiving, and her voice breaking out now and again into melody. Sometimes it was the words of some old hymn or of a well-known and much-loved text. They set themselves to music without an effort on her part.

On, still on, Mary went, heeding not the length and weariness of the way. The afternoon came and went. The sun set in the western heavens with a glory that made

Mary Jones' Bible

Mary think of the home prepared above for God's children. In her mind she could see heaven with its walls of jasper, and its gates of pearl, and its streets of gold, and its light that needs neither sun nor moon, but streams from the Life-giving Presence of God Himself.

That evening Jacob and his wife were seated, waiting for supper and for Mary. What news would their daughter bring? Had she reached Bala safely? Had she received her Bible? These were just some of the questions which the anxious parents asked themselves, listening the while for their daughter's return after the tiring and possibly dangerous efforts of her fifty miles' walk.

But the caring couple were not long kept in suspense.

Presently the step, which they knew so well, approached the cottage. The latch was lifted. Mary entered, weary, footsore, dusty and travel-stained. But she entered with happiness dimpling her cheeks and flashing in her eyes. And Jacob held out both arms to his daughter and as he clasped her to his heart, he murmured, "Is all well?" and Mary, from the depths of a satisfied heart, answered with gladness, "All is well."

It so often happens that when a person has wanted something for a long time, possessing it does not bring the happiness expected. Interest in the treasure is quickly lost. It was not so, however, with Mary Jones.

The Bible for which she had toiled, and waited, and prayed, and wept, became each day more precious to her. Chapter after chapter was learned by heart, and the study of the Sunday school lessons became her greatest privilege and delight.

Now, if a question was asked by the teacher, which other girls could not answer, Mary was always appealed to, and always seemed ready with a thoughtful intelligent reply. In committing to memory not only chapters, but whole books of the Bible, Mary was unrivalled both in the Sunday school and neighborhood.

Nor was this all. For though to love, and read, and learn the Bible are good things, Mary knew it was Jesus who said, "Os cerwch fi, cedwch fy ngorchymynion. Ac mi a weddiaf ar y Tad, ac efe a rydd i chwi Ddiddanydd arall, fel yr aroso gyd a chwi yn dragywyddol." ("If you love Me, you will obey My commandments. I will ask the Father, and He will give you another Helper, who will stay with you for ever" John 14:15-16).

Her mother, who had at one time feared that Mary's longing to possess a Bible of her own might lead her to neglect her practical duties, was surprised and delighted to see that, although there was a change indeed in the girl, it was a change for the better. The Holy Spirit was filling her life and teaching her.

The truths that sank into Mary's heart were the precious seed in good ground, which "brings forth fruit a hundredfold". Mary found that there was pleasure in the commonest duties of life, because they were done for the Lord.

Not very long after her visit to Bala, Mary had the great pleasure of seeing again the kind friend with whom, in her memory, her Bible would now always be associated.

Thomas Charles, in the course of his visits to the various villages where his schools were established, came to Abergynolwyn, to inspect the school there, which was

Monument to Mr. Charles at Bala

still under the charge of Lewis Williams. Mr. Charles would talk with the children personally, to assure himself of their progress.

Among the bright young faces upturned to him, his observant eye soon caught sight of one that he had cause to remember with special and with deep interest. The interest deepened still more when he found that from her alone all his most difficult questions received replies.

Thomas Charles did not miss this opportunity of saying a few encouraging words to his young friend, and Mary in her turn treasured them up, and remembered them through the many years and the various events of her life.

CHAPTER 8

The Work Begun

There is no doubt that Mary's determined effort to obtain a Bible made a deep impression upon the mind and heart of Thomas Charles. Often he thought of that bare-footed girl, her weary journey, and her eagerness to spend her six years' savings on the purchase of a Bible. Then the bitter tears of disappointment, and the sweet tears of joy—all these came back to his recollection again and again. They came blended with the memory of the ignorance and darkness of too many of his countrymen. It seem to Thomas Charles that a cry was going up all over Wales for the Word of God. There were times when he thought of nothing else.

In the winter of 1802 Thomas Charles visited London, full of one great thought and plan, though not seeing how it could be carried out.

It was while turning the matter over in his mind one morning, that the idea occurred to him of a society for the Scriptures. A society set up to publish and distribute God's Holy Word.

Consulting with some of his friends who belonged to the Committee of the Religious Tract Society, he received the warmest encouragement. At their next meeting he spoke about Wales and its lack of Bibles, bringing forward the story of Mary Jones to give extra power to his appeal on behalf of his Welsh countrymen.

Nor was the appeal without effect. A wave of sympathy for the people that so longed and thirsted for the Word of God, ran through the assembled meeting. A great desire took hold of Thomas Charles's hearers to do something towards supplying the great need. The hearts of many were further stirred when one of the secretaries of the Committee, the Reverend Joseph Hughes, rose, and in reply to Mr. Charles' appeal for Bibles for Wales, exclaimed enthusiastically,

"Mr. Charles, surely a society might be formed for the purpose; and if for Wales, why not for the world?"

This immediately found an echo in the hearts of many in the audience. So the secretary was instructed to prepare a letter inviting Christians everywhere, of all denominations, to unite in forming a society for spreading God's Word over the whole earth.

Two years passed while plans were made. Then in the month of March, 1804, the British and Foreign Bible Society was started, and at its first meeting the sum of £700 was raised, which was a large amount in those days.

Unfortunately Mr. Charles was unable to be present at this meeting. He was hard at work at home in Wales, but he heard the news with the greatest joy. It was owing to his work and to that of his friends, as well as to the efforts of other Christian workers who deeply felt the great need of the people at this time, that the contributions in Wales alone soon amounted to nearly £1,900. Most of this sum did not come from the rich, but from the poorer people who were now showing their love for the Lord and for their neighbors.

In the Bible Society all denominations helped, brought together by a common cause, and a great wish to serve one common Master. Representatives of the Christian Churches were working together for the good and enlightenment of the world, by bringing people to know and love Jesus.

Meanwhile, Mr. Charles was even busier at work. Wherever he told the true story, either in Welsh or English meetings, of the young girl of Llanfihangel, the simple narrative never failed to carry home some lessons to the heart of each hearer.

Great was the joy and thankfulness of this hard-working minister of Christ, when he learnt that the first work of the Committee of the Bible Society would be to bring out an edition of the Welsh Bible for use in Welsh Sunday schools. And his delight was greater still when the first consignment of these Bibles reached Bala in 1806.

"Beibl i bawd o bobl y byd'—"a Bible to all the people of earth" became a popular saying amongst Welsh Christians.

On leaving school Mary Jones worked as a weaver, while still living with her parents. Her precious Bible was as dear to her as ever.

Mary was intensely interested in the founding of the Bible Society, and in the news of the first edition of the new Welsh Bibles arriving at Bala.

But in addition to her weaving, and the household help she gave her mother, who was now neither well nor strong, Mary had become good at dressmaking. This

stood her in good stead when she wished to earn a little extra money.

All who could afford it came to her to cut out and make their dresses, and though Mary never wasted a moment, she sometimes found it quite difficult to do during the day all that she had planned.

As for Jacob, his chest was weaker through asthma. When the winter winds and heavy mists came, his sufferings were very great. But he bore his affliction—bore it, as he said, "for the dear Lord's sake," who had borne so much for him.

Occasionally Mr.Charles would visit Abergynolwyn, and every now and then Llanfihangel. At such times he and Mary Jones met again, and she would learn from him how the Society in London was going on—that great London which was a strange, distant, untried world to her. She had only vague ideas of its size and its distance from the little, quiet, secluded place where she lived.

All the while, up in London, the great tree of life went on growing and spreading. And the root from which it had sprung—Mary Jones—remained in Wales, almost unseen. God was showing that He had need of the high and the lowly, the great and the small.

Out of all, and *through* all, and *in* all, He works His wondrous way, and permits His people to join with Him in turning the world from darkness to His marvellous light.

CHAPTER 9

The Work Goes On

When next we visit Llanfihangel, Mary is no longer Mary Jones. A great change has come over her surroundings. Her school work and her old home life with her parents are things of the past.

She has married a weaver, Thomas Lewis by name, and is living at the village of Bryncrug, near Tywyn, not very far from Llanfihangel. But all this has not changed the character of Mary, save as the advancing summer may be said to change the fruit by ripening it.

This has been a sad time for Mary, as well as a happy one. Jacob and Molly Jones, who had brought her up to know and love the Lord and Savior, were dead. But Mary knew that in heaven her parents were happy, and for them all suffering and unhappiness was in the past.

So here at Bryncrug, with a husband and children of her own, with new duties, and fresh cares, Mary's love for her Bible was still growing.

Other things had changed—friends, home influences, claims, interests—but God's Word remained to her unaltered, except that every day it grew more into her heart, and became more one with her life. From careful study, and prayer for God's Spirit to open her eyes to deeper meanings, Mary discovered truths in the Bible which had been unnoticed by her before.

Mary's life had been a busy one during the years spent at Llanfihangel, but doubly so was her life here at Bryncrug. Yet for all her hard work, Mary had a way of making every duty, however humble and simple, a service for Jesus. So, by her Christian life she influenced the people she met from day to day.

If a neighbor's child wished to have a Sunday school lesson explained, she invariably came to Mary, who could always spare a few minutes to give the same instruction that had been so precious to her in her childhood days. And Mary's good knowledge of the Bible gave her a very clear way of explaining its truths. She was now a wise counsellor and teacher.

If, again, a friend wanted a hint or two in making a new dress, or advice over the management of her bee hives, Mary was always the authority appealed to. She was known as the most capable, as well as the kindest of neighbors, and ever ready to lend a helping hand, or speak a helpful word.

So, in Bryncrug, Mary was winning the love and confidence of her neighbors and showing in her life and character the love of the Savior whose faithful servant she tried to be.

Bryncrug

Mary was certainly an authority on bees, as her success with her own bee hives proved. That success was simply remarkable, both in the large number of hives, and their profitable results.

The power and influence which Mary seemed to exercise over people appeared to extend even to her bees. Whenever she went near the hives, her reception by her winged subjects was nothing less than royal.

The air would be thick with buzzing swarms, and presently they would alight upon her by hundreds, covering her from head to foot, walking over her, but never attempting to sting, or showing any feeling but one of absolute friendliness. She would even catch a handful of them, but softly, so as not to hurt them. They never misunderstood her, or gave her the slightest injury. In short, there seemed to be some close understanding between Mary and her bees, and they were the means of earning money to go towards the support of God's work in the world.

The money brought by the sale of the honey was used for the family and household expenses, but the money from the sale of the wax was divided among the Christian societies which, poor as the family was, Mary wanted to help.

Among these, foremost in her estimation stood the British and Foreign Bible Society. She had been closely connected with the founding of the Society, and she was never happier than when she could spare what for her was a large sum, to help in sending the Word of God— so precious to her own heart—over the world.

Mary was also very interested in the Calvinistic Methodist Missionary Society—a Society founded by the denomination to which she had, for so many years, belonged. Secretly she gave up many things so there would be money to spare for the work of the Gospel.

On one occasion, when a collection was made at Bryncrug for the China Million Testament Fund in 1854, a gold coin—a half sovereign—was found in the collection plate. It was neatly wrapped up between two copper half-pence, and thus hidden until the money came to be counted.

This was Mary's gift, the gift of a loving and generous heart touched both by God's love, and by the spiritual needs of people throughout the world.

Mary was sitting at her cottage door one day, when a neighbor, Betsy Davies, came up.

"Hello, Mary," she said, "may I sit with you this afternoon? I've a dress I am altering for my eldest girl, and I don't see how to finish it. I thought maybe you'd be good enough to show me."

"Yes, of course I will, with pleasure," replied Mary. "My children are all at school, and my husband has gone to Tywyn, so I have a quiet hour or two before me. Let me see your work, Betsy."

Betsy Davies laid the dress over Mary's knee, and Mary's eyes, quick and intelligent as ever, saw in a moment or two what was needed.

"That's not a difficult job," she said pleasantly, if nor a long one. Just unpick that seam, Betsy, and I'll pin it for you as it ought to be. Then if you let down the tuck in the skirt, you'll have it long enough; and as for that torn part, I think I've got some thread about the right color to darn it up. I will show you how I darn my young daughter's dresses when she tears them, as she does very often, playing with her brothers. Yours can be mended in the same way, and you'll see it will hardly show at all."

When the two women had settled down to their work, Betsy said, "I wish you'd tell me, Mary, how you manage to get on as you do. You can't be rich people. Your husband is a weaver like mine—like most of the others here. Yet you never get into debt, and you always seem to have enough for yourselves. And what's more amazing still, you've enough to give something away too! I must say I can't understand it!"

"I don't think there's anything very hard to understand," said Mary, smiling. "If by being careful, and giving some things up, we can help in God's work, it is surely the greatest joy we can have."

"Yes, that's all very well," replied Betsy, "but I never have anything to give. Yet I haven't as many children as you, and so my family and housekeeping doesn't cost so much."

"It's like this, Betsy," said Mary; "we ask ourselves 'What can I do without?' And each of us in the family is willing to give up some little luxury, and so we save the money. We put it into a box which we call the treasury. Then, whenever we add anything to what we keep there, we think of the widow who dropped her two mites into the treasury of the temple and how Jesus said such loving words about her."

Writing in the Bible, by Mary Jones,
when she had learnt some English

"But what *sort* of things can you give up?" asked Betsy. "We poor folk, it seems to me, don't have any more than just the necessities of life. We can't give up eating, or go without clothes to our backs."

"That is true," agreed Mary. "But I think if you consider a bit, you'll see there are some things which are not really essential, though they may be pleasant. Now for instance, Thomas had always been used to a pipe and a bit of tobacco in an evening after his work was done. But when we were all wondering what we could give up for our Lord's sake he said, 'I'll give up my smoke in the evenings.' And I tell you, Betsy, the tears came into my eyes when I heard that, knowing that my husband's words meant a real sacrifice. Then our eldest son, wishing to follow his father's example, cried out, 'And I've still got the Christmas money I was given last winter, and I'll give that.' And Sally, she gave up the thought of a new hat ribbon I'd promised her, and she sponged and ironed her old one instead, and wore it, feeling prouder than if it had been new. And as for little Benny, he was all day picking up sticks in the woods to earn a penny, and that was *his gift.*"

"And you yourself?" asked Betsy, with interest.

"I? Oh, I have the wax that my bees make. The money I get by selling that goes into the treasury, as well as any other small sum I do not *really* need. And I must say, Betsy, we have never really suffered for the want of anything that we have given to God. He repays us with such happiness and content as He alone can give."

"That I can well believe," agreed Betsy, "for I never hear you grumble, or see you look cross or discontented like so many of the neighbors—as I do myself only too often. Well, Mary," she continued, "I mean to try your plan, though it will come very hard at first, as I'm not used to that sort of saving."

"I think I got used to it when I was just a girl, putting away my little mites of money towards buying a Bible." answered Mary. "For six years I put aside all my money, and since then it has come natural."

"You did get your Bible, then?"

"Yes, indeed; this is the very one." Rising from her seat Mary took the much prized volume from the table in the cottage, and put it into her neighbor's hands.

Betsy looked at it, inside and out, then handed it back saying, "I really believe, Mary, that this Bible is one of the reasons why you are so different from all the rest of us. You've read, and studied, and learnt so much of it, that your thoughts and words and life are full of it. "And Mary turned her bright dark eyes, now full of happy tears towards her companion. "Oh, Betsy dear, if there is a little, even a little truth in what you say of me, I thank God. Even now I am surprised that He allows me, poor and weak though I am, to show to others the truths of His Word.

"And, Betsy, He *wants* me to do it. He needs us all. Perhaps we will never understand just how much we are needed. It was Jesus the Son of God who said,

" 'Onid ydych chwi yn dywedyd, Y mae etto bedwar mis, ac *yna* y daw'r cynhauaf? Wele, yr ydwyf fi yn dywedyd wrthych, Derchefwch eich llygaid, ac edrychwch ar y maesydd; canys gwynion ydynt eisoes i'r cynhauaf.' "

Ruins of Mary Jones' cottage
(in 1882)

("You have a saying, 'Four more months and then the harvest.' But I tell you, take a good look at the fields; the crops are now ripe and ready to be harvested!" John 4:35).

"And who is going to reap the harvest for God if you and I don't do it, Betsy? Who *will* be a laborer for the Lord?"

Mary Jones's Bible.

The case in the Bible House